Robbie's Dillydally,
Willy-Nilly,
Shilly-Shally
Letter to Santa Claus

Edward Ronny Arnold

Illustrated by Aya Suarjaya

Computer Classics ®
Nashville, Tennessee

This is a work of fiction. Names, characters, places, and incidents are used fictitiously. Any resemblance to actual persons, living or dead, events, or locales is entirely coincidental.

Illustrations - Artwork by Aya Suarjaya.

ISBN: 978099265-6-0

Library of Congress Control Number: 2018902652

Chapters

Disappointing Christmas

"Thank you, Santa."

The words, if written, looked and sounded nice; courteous. Spoken, they had the same excitement as shuffling a deck of cards. The words were a formality, a common ritual performed each Christmas morning; with no real meaning or actual emotional feel of a thank you.

A pleasant game, handing out presents on Christmas morning, was nothing more than a yearly disappointment for Robert. He felt the package, small, squishy, a wallet? He did not need one; he had one, the same present he received last year. Opening the package, the green canvas wallet with a Velcro fastener looked too thick; slowly opening it in hope, no money. "Thank you, Santa," he muttered.

The other gifts followed: two neckties, cologne, socks, a book; nothing he really wanted, "Thank you, Santa."

His wife Marsha and their three adopted children, Barry, Nicholas, and Kara, got what they wanted: toys, clothes, and money. Robert never got what he wanted. He reached into his pants pocket and felt the letter. It was a copy of a letter he wrote when he was nine years-old, fifty-seven years ago in the year 1960. He wrote the same letter to Santa Claus for six years. Santa never delivered. Sighing sadly, he walked into the kitchen and poured himself a cup of coffee. Feeling like the character Ebenezer Scrooge from Charles Dickens' *A Christmas Carol*, Christmas was a humbug.

Disappointment, that was what Robert experienced every Christmas morning. He knew what to expect under the tree from Santa, nothing he really wanted. Oh, the toy train was nice when he was nine and he rode the bicycle he received at the age of ten but it was not what he wanted; it was not what he asked for. He felt the letter in his pocket, "Humbug."

"Did you have another disappointing Christmas?" Sandra, the waitress at Cracker Barrel asked. Robert nodded his head, as he sipped coffee.

"Maybe next year?" she asked.

"Doubtful," Robert answered.

"What happened?" a man sitting at the next table asked.

Robert shrugged his shoulders.

"Robert wrote a letter to Santa Claus many years ago," Sandra answered. "He has been waiting for Santa to deliver, but Santa never delivers."

"Not yet," Robert said. "I still have faith in Santa. Perhaps what I asked for is too much."

"What's that?" the man asked.

"A pony," Sandra answered. "Robert wrote Santa asking for a pony when he was nine years-old and he never received it." She snickered.

The man howled with laughter. He giggled as he moved his plate and coffee cup from his table to sit opposite of Robert. "You do not understand the issues of your request," the man said. "Your request does not make any sense to Santa. That is why he has not delivered."

"What issues?" Robert asked.

"Food for the pony, a saddle and a bridle," the man answered. "Also, there is the issue of delivery space on the sleigh. In addition, there are restrictions in the city for what animals can be kept. You have to consider the cost of an annual rabies shot and a collar." He sipped his coffee and laughed. "A pony is not allowed to wander freely in the city and you have to walk it on a leash and pick up any droppings."

Sandra laughed.

"I asked for food and a saddle," Robert muttered. "Ponies are not required to have rabies shots or a collar. The idea is to ride them not walk them."

"Hum," the man muttered. He reached into his coat pocket and removed a business card. "I am a lawyer and I think this is a possible legal suit."

"Sue Santa Claus?" Sandra asked. "That's different."

"Not Santa Claus, the United States Post Office," the man answered. "My name is Eric Jordan, Attorney at Law. The suit is not against Santa it is against the United States Post Office... depending."

Robert took the business card and he looked at it. "Depending on what?"

"Did you mail it?" Eric asked. "Did you address the letter and place a stamp on it?"

"Yes," Robert answered. "I personally placed it in the mailbox. What difference does it make?"

"Obvious," Eric answered. "You never received the pony because the United States Post Office failed to comply with their duty and deliver it. You never got the pony because the Post Office never delivered the letter.

Santa never got it! The Post Office is liable. They owe you a pony and whatever goes with it."

"A cowboy hat, two six guns with lots of paper caps, and cowboy boots," Robert said.

Sandra laughed. "You asked Santa for a cowboy hat, guns, boots, and a pony?"

Robert frowned. "Roy Rogers was the King of the Cowboys when I was nine. I wrote Santa a letter asking for a Roy Rogers' hat, guns, boots and a pony that looked like Trigger." He grinned. "Trigger was the smartest horse in the movies." He sipped his coffee. "I also asked for lots of paper cap ammunition to chase the bad guys out of town and a saddle and food for little Trigger."

"Reasonable request considering the times," Eric said. "My initial fee is five hundred dollars and we have a legal action against the United States Post Office."

Sandra laughed as Eric winked at her.

"I can file the motion next Monday in Federal Court," he continued. "If we do go to court, and I do not think we will, my fee is one thousand dollars."

"Do you think we will win?" Robert asked.

"There are no guarantees," Eric answered. "However, we have sound legal arguments and the Post Office will probably settle rather than spend the money on a protracted legal battle. We have questions they are not prepared to answer."

"I will think about it," Robert said. He paid his bill, left a tip, and walked out of the restaurant.

When Robert left the restaurant, Eric looked at Sandra. "That was fun. Who is he?"

"He is a very nice person," Sandra answered. "He and his family come into the restaurant about once a week for breakfast. They are older but they adopted three young children, two boys and a girl. I have known him for three years and he always comes in the day after Christmas. He is sad and tells me about his disappointing Christmas, no pony."

Sandra refilled Eric's coffee cup. "Are you a real lawyer?" Sandra asked.

"Yes," Eric answered, with a sigh. "But I am not a good one. I was fired from my job because I was told I am not mean enough. Right now I am working out of my home."

"Are you going to actually file a legal suit?" Sandra asked.

"Sure," Eric answered. "The case has merits." He smiled slightly. "You seem like a nice person. Are you attached?"

"No," Sandra answered smiling. "Are you attached?"

"No," Eric answered. "I was but my girlfriend left me when I was fired." He shrugged his shoulders. "If you accept a date with me I warn you, everyone says I am a nice person."

"Just my type," Sandra said smiling. "I get off work at 2:00 P.M. There is a movie I would like to see and since you do not have a job, I will pay."

Done Deal

"Why are we meeting in a restaurant?" Robert asked. He was sitting in a small sandwich shop located near the mall.

"I do not have an office, just yet," Eric answered. "I am currently working out of my home and it is messy. This is more private."

"It looks more public than private," Robert said. He pushed a sealed envelope toward Eric. "I did as you asked, cash, all twenties."

Eric wrote a receipt and handed it to Robert. "The legal brief is almost done. I will file it Monday morning."

"What happens?" Robert asked.

"Nothing really," Eric answered. "The court receives it, a copy of the suit is sent to the Defendant and a judge is assigned. There will be a preliminary hearing."

"What is that?" Robert asked. "Do I take the witness stand and testify?"

"No," Eric answered. "The two attorneys argue a portion of our cases. The judge asks questions and then sets a trial date. The only evidence we will present is that copy of a letter you wrote and mailed in the year 1960. I need the original. It will be included with the brief and we keep copies."

Robert handed Eric a large manila envelope. "Here it is. I made ten copies. Do I get my original back? I would like to keep it."

Eric paused. "You will owe me additional money at the trial." He paused again. "Does your wife know?"

"Yes, I told her," Robert answered. "She was not happy at first but she understands. Marsha wants me to be happy and she understands. I have told her many times about the pony."

"Yes," Eric said slowly. "The Post Office does not want this type of publicity and they will settle." He held his right hand outward, "Done deal?"

"Sure!" Robert said excited as he shook hands. "I can't wait to get my pony."

Robbie vs.
The United States Postal Service

"Do you know how ridiculous this is?" Judge Benson asked Eric. He laughed as he read the brief: *Robbie's Dillydally, Willy-Nilly, Shilly-Shally Letter to Santa Claus.*

"It is not ridiculous," Eric answered. "The United States Post Office has a legal, binding contract with every person who places a stamp on a letter and mails it."

"Objection," the attorney for the United States Post Office said, "A frivolous suit. The statute of limitations has run out. The United States Post Office has no liability regarding delivery for a letter written fifty-seven years ago."

"You're Honor," Eric said. "The regulations of the United States Postal Service do not state any statute of limitation for delivery. In fact, many years ago, a letter was discovered unprocessed and mishandled for forty-four years. The Postal Service delivered the letter and received positive publicity for fulfilling its duty, forty-four years later."

Judge Benson smiled and he leaned backward in his chair, obviously enjoying the show. "Objection overruled. What was the postal rate to deliver a letter to the North Pole in the year 1960?"

"I have no idea," the attorney answered. "The domestic Letter Rate in the year 1960 was four cents per ounce. Postcard Rate: three cents. Air Mail Rate: seven cents per ounce. The main stamp issued was the Pony Express Centennial Stamp from Sacramento, California. They were first issued July 19, 1960. One hundred nineteen million six hundred sixty-five thousand were printed. The Post Office is prepared to refund Robert his four cents, with interest. The total amount is three dollars and nineteen cents."

Judge Benson smiled. "Is the United States Post Office prepared to refund the postage, with interest, to every child who wrote a letter to Santa Claus that was never delivered?"

"Of course not," the attorney answered. "We have no idea of how many children wrote letters to Santa."

"This case is not about the cost of a stamp," Eric said. "It is about delivery. If the Post Office delivered the letter, little nine year-old Robbie would have received his pony. The Post Office is liable for the pony, accessories, and my legal fees."

"You're Honor," the attorney said irritated. "The Post Office is fully aware of its responsibility to deliver mail. However, each December more than three hundred thousand letters are written to Santa Claus. Of those many letters, some have no address, just a name." He walked to a table and picked up a sheet of paper. "Last year, less than four hundred letters had a stamp. Of those four hundred, less than two hundred had an address. That address was Santa Claus, North Pole." He walked toward the bench. "The attorney for the Plaintiff has offered no evidence his client placed a stamp and an address where the letter could be delivered. All he has presented as evidence is a copy of a letter written to Santa Claus fifty-seven years ago."

Eric smiled. "You're Honor, the attorney just told this court they had no idea how many children wrote letters to Santa, then he gave a number."

"Exactly," the attorney said. "Children write letters to Santa but never mail them. We know how many are processed but not actually written. Those letters that cannot be delivered are placed in the Dead Letter Section."

Eric smiled. "So, you dillydally with the letters."

The attorney looked puzzled. "I do not know what dillydally is."

"You treat them willy-nilly," Eric said.

The attorney looked puzzled. "I do not know what willy-nilly is."

"You treat them shilly-shally," Eric said.

The attorney looked more puzzled. "I do not know what shilly-shally is."

"You're Honor," Eric said. "The attorney for the Defendant just stated he treated Robbie's letter to Santa Claus in a dillydally, willy-nilly, shilly-shally manner by placing his letter in the Dead Letter Section. He admitted the Post Office treated Robbie's letter, and all children's letters written to Santa Claus, slowly, without care, callous and unconcerned."

"What?" the attorney asked. "I admitted nothing. You're Honor, the United States Post Office takes its fiduciary duty seriously." He looked at his watch. "In order to solve this issue, the United States Post Office, with full cooperation of the United States Air Force, will fulfill its obligation to the Plaintiff within the next thirty minutes."

"Robbie gets his pony and I get my legal fees?" Eric asked excited.

"Hardly," the attorney answered. "The Plaintiff claims he wrote a letter to Santa Claus addressed to the North Pole and placed a stamp. The letter had no street name, house number or possible forwarding address. There were no zip codes in the year 1960." He looked at Eric. "Santa could have moved. We have no record of a Mr. Santa Claus filing a forwarding address. Therefore, effective immediately, the United States Post Office will have an Air Force plane drop all letters addressed to Santa Claus, North Pole, with a cancelled stamp, at the North Pole. Robbie's belated letter is first." He looked at his watch. "The letter should be dropped within the next thirty minutes. However, the North Pole is a very big place. It does not matter where it is dropped."

"That is not a solution!" Eric yelled. "You are liable! Robbie gets his pony and I get my legal fees."

"We are not liable for anything!" the attorney yelled. He smiled. "We will deliver the letter. It is up to Santa Claus to decide to fill the request." He paused. "However, only those letters postmarked by December 20 will be air dropped; to give Santa time to fill them."

"No! No!" Eric yelled. "You owe Robert a pony and you owe me legal fees!"

Judge Benson smiled and laughed loudly, tapping his gavel. "I am afraid I will have to rule with the United States Post Office. If they are willing to deliver the Plaintiff's letter, this case can be dismissed. If the letter is delivered, it is Santa's decision to fill it. However, this case cannot be dismissed until after December 25."

He tapped his gavel. "This case is adjourned until December 26."

The people in the courtroom stood as Judge Benson stood and walked from his bench. He laughed loudly as he opened his private door and exited the courtroom.

"What happened?" Robert asked Eric as he sat down.

"You never know what a person wearing a black robe will do," Eric answered. "They are going to deliver your letter and the man in the black robe effectively dismissed the suit."

"Do I get my pony?" Robert asked.

"Doubtful," Eric answered as he packed his briefcase. "I will telephone you in a few days. You owe me money for filing fees and I will prepare your bill." He paused. "Sorry."

Eric was leaving the courtroom when Sandra stopped him. "What happened? You said the Post Office was going to get Robert a pony and pay your legal fees."

"There is no pony or money," Eric answered. "The Post Office is going to deliver the letter and the judge dismissed the case. We are to appear in court December 26 but there is no need." He looked sad. "Sorry, I did my best but I failed Robbie and every child who ever wrote a letter to Santa Claus."

Sandra smiled and hugged Eric. "I am very proud of you! I thought you were wonderful and you should have won." They held hands as they walked out of the courtroom.

One of the reporters covering the case laughed. "What a joke, a waste of my time." He was holding several sheets of paper where he wrote notes from the preliminary hearing and crumbled them.

Another reporter laughed. "I agree. If we print this, every child in the United States will put a stamp on their letter. The Air Force will be using valuable planes to drop hundreds of thousands of letters at the North Pole." He laughed again. "My report goes into the Dead Article File; the trash can. I will treat my report of this court case exactly like the United States Post Office treated nine year-old Robbie's letter; dillydally, willy-nilly and shilly-shally."

Robert slowly stood. He watched as everyone began to leave the courtroom.

Special Delivery to Santa Claus

"How much further?" the pilot asked the copilot.

"About ten minutes," the copilot answered. "We will be over the North Pole in ten minutes."

The pilot looked outward; there was nothing to see except white snow and ice. "Do you believe in Santa Claus?"

"No," the copilot answered. "I never received what I asked for. I asked Santa for a real submarine and a real rocket ship. I wanted to go to Mars and see the little green men." He laughed. "What did you ask for?"

"A train set," the pilot answered. "I wrote a letter to Santa asking for a Lionel train set and nailed it to the wall beside the Christmas tree. I wanted lots of track, a toy bridge, a toy tunnel, a toy farm house, toy animals and toy people." He grinned slightly. "I got it! I was awakened Christmas morning to the sound of a train whistle. Santa set up the train and it was running around the tree. That's all I got but that was all I asked for. Santa delivered."

The navigator laughed. "I never received what I asked for. I wanted a real dragon. I wanted it to fly and breathe fire. There was this boy in school I did not like named William. William was always mean to me and I wanted the dragon to scare him." He laughed. "I was going to name the dragon Mr. Mean. I must have been on Santa's naughty list because Santa never delivered."

The pilot and copilot laughed.

The navigator frowned at the pilot. "This whole mission is silly. I would rather be at the base watching television. Why are you so happy?"

"This is exciting!" the pilot answered. "I told my eight year-old son his father was delivering a special delivery letter to Santa Claus at the North Pole. He was very excited and told his friends at school. It was Sam's suggestion I add the parachute and flashing lights to the box so Santa could find it."

He laughed loudly. "His third grade teacher, Mrs. Elmore, was also excited when Sam told her I was delivering mail to Santa Claus. She sent e-mails to every teacher she knows to have them instruct the children to address their letters to Santa Claus, North Pole. If they place a stamp on it, the Post Office will have the United States Air Force deliver their letter to Santa Claus December 20."

The pilot smiled proudly. "Mrs. Elmore also wrote in her e-mails one or more requests should not be selfish. The children should think of someone less fortunate and ask Santa for something that person needs."

"That is real good," the copilot said. "Sam's teacher is very smart. She is using the mail run to teach children to not be selfish."

"That is a wonderful idea, teaching children not to be selfish at Christmas," the navigator said. "Now that I think about it, this is exciting! You do realize we are making history."

"What history?" the copilot asked.

"The first United States Air Force air mail drop to Santa Claus at the North Pole," the navigator answered proudly.

"That is exciting," the copilot laughed.

"Hum," the navigator muttered. "I am going to volunteer for the December 20 mail run."

"Why?" the pilot asked. "You always take vacation the week before Christmas."

"I will just change the dates slightly," the navigator answered. "I go home every year for Christmas. I do not have children but I enjoy my sister's two young children. My nieces Ellen and Janice will really be surprised when I tell them I was a part of the first and second United States Air Force teams that delivered mail to Santa Claus at the North Pole. My participation in the two mail runs was very important. The letters we delivered, written by children to Santa, included an unselfish request." He paused and smiled proudly. "I am one of Santa's helpers."

"Good idea," the copilot said. "I want to be one of Santa's helpers also. I can't wait to tell the children in my daughter's elementary school I delivered mail to Santa Claus at the North Pole, twice!" He laughed loudly. "Every child in her school will bring me a letter to deliver to Santa but I will refuse to accept their letter unless it contains one unselfish request. When we return to the base, I will volunteer all of us. How much further?"

"We are almost there," the navigator answered laughing. "We are more than thirty miles from the exact location of the North Pole, ninety degrees north. However, there is turbulence ahead and we are close enough." He pressed a button and the hydraulic system activated causing the third cargo bay door to slowly open. As it opened wider, a metallic box, one foot wide by one foot long, four inches deep, slid outward. The box fell out of the cargo bay as a parachute opened slowing the fall. The box drifted gently downward and came to rest on the snow with red, blue and green lights flashing.

The pilot pressed a button and spoke into his headset, "Letter to Santa Claus delivered." Laughing loudly and moving the controls, the plane made a slow left turn south, headed toward Anchorage, Alaska.

"I know someone who can make us jackets to wear for the mail run," the navigator said. "The jackets will have our first names on it and the date."

The pilot laughed loud. "The Santa Claus Mail Run! Embroidered on the back will be our first names and Ninety Degrees North!"

"Red! Red!" the copilot said excited. "They have to be red because Santa always wears red! Don't forget to add Santa's Helper above our first name. Our names need to be on the front below Santa's Helper. On the back will be Santa Claus Mail Run, Ninety Degrees North and the date, December 20, 2018."

"Dashing through the sky, in a four engine Globemaster III," they began to sing. "Over clouds we go, laughing all the way. Bells on flight decks ring, making spirits bright. What fun it is to ride and sing a flying song today."

The navigator interrupted the song. "We are singing off key," he said seriously.

The box rested on the snow with the three colored lights flashing. A small red-gloved hand appeared out of nowhere. The hand came from underneath a garment. The garment was white, the same color as the snow and covered an elf. The white garment was used for concealment. Pushing the garment backward, Creasy the elf looked at the box. Creasy was three feet tall and wore a red pointed hat, red shirt, red coat, red pants and red shoes. His elfin ears were covered with red colored ear muffs. His skin color was a pale brown and his eyes were dark in color. The length of his white beard indicated his age; one hundred fourteen years, nine days, sixteen minutes and twelve seconds.

Picking the box upward, he noticed an electrical switch on the side. Moving the switch, the three colored lights stopped flashing. Written on the outside of the box in a black marker was a name and address: Santa Claus, North Pole. Carefully rolling the parachute around the box, he clutched it tightly.

Replacing the white cover, Creasy walked north. He walked an estimated one mile when he approached a large snow drift. Moving a section of cloth that covered the snow drift, he entered one of the many concealed entrances. Santa's workshop and home was built below the surface, not above. The tall snow drift was only used for entrance and exit. The far side contained one of the many loading docks and runways for Santa and his sleigh.

Placing his concealment cloth on a hanger, with the others, he walked casually toward a large wooden box. Entering the box, he pushed a lever and the box descended downward into the main shop. The shop was not busy as the month was February and the day was Tuesday. Elves moved slowly preparing toys for children. The toys were mainly made of wood: toy soldier nut crackers, dolls and doll furniture. Their main business was making candy and fruitcakes. Christmas changed over the years. Creasy watched with sadness as children asked Santa for more expensive, elaborate toys. Gone were the requests for simple things: dolls, and doll houses, doll furniture, stuffed animals, toy soldiers, paper cap guns and train sets. Children now asked for videos, expensive sports shoes, starter sports team jackets, computers, high definition television sets and portable telephones. He sighed as he walked toward one of the older elves.

"Special delivery for Santa," he said. "A United States military airplane, C-17 Globemaster III, serial number AK-19-POLAR9 with three crew members named Justin, Harold, and John just dropped it." He shrugged his shoulders. "I could hear a slight noise. The left hydraulic control on the third rear cargo bay door is .004 PSI low on pressure.

The left coupler connection needs to be tightened .0009 millimeters. It is not dangerous but the flight mechanics need to have it corrected."

He shrugged his shoulders again. "It doesn't make any difference but they changed the lyrics to *Jingle Bells*. The words bright and today do not rhyme and they are all singing the new song off key."

"Who is it from?" the older elf named Thriddle asked. He was also dressed in red and the length of his beard indicated his age; one hundred and sixty-two years, three days, twenty-two minutes and eighteen seconds.

"I do not know," Creasy answered. "I did not open it. It is addressed to Santa. Where is he?"

"Private quarters," Thriddle answered. "He is depressed. It is February... post-Christmas let down."

Creasy walked through the main shop, turned left, passed the kitchen, passed the dining hall and stopped at a door. Knock. Knock. "Special delivery for Santa," he said quietly.

The door opened as Mrs. Santa Claus smiled. "Santa has a special delivery in February? This may cheer him up. Please come inside."

Mrs. Claus smiled cheerfully as she opened the door wider. She was wearing a very ornate red dress. The sleeves were trimmed in a white cloth and she was wearing a red hat over her long white hair. "He is over here sitting in his chair." She walked toward the left as Creasy followed holding the metallic box. "Santa, you have a special delivery package."

Santa's private quarters were very simple. The main room was composed of two large chairs that faced a fireplace. There was no fire as it was not cold in the Arctic in February. A large mantle, made of stone, covered the entrance. Placed on the mantle were many photographs taken of Mr. and Mrs. Claus through the years. One hundred fifteen were not photographs but drawings and paintings. A large desk was placed to the side, where Santa prepared his list of good children. Large reams of paper were stacked neatly beside the desk and the nice list, so far, was short; less than eight nautical miles in length.

Santa sat in his chair looking at the darkened fireplace. He was wearing his red pants and black boots. Santa's signature red coat and hat were placed on a hanger to the side. He wore a red long-sleeve shirt and his pants were held upward with wide black suspenders. Santa's long beard had been recently trimmed. It came to his chest and matched his recently trimmed white hair and long bushy, white eyebrows.

Santa was depressed. It was the annual post-Christmas let down. Many children no longer believed in him and his nice list was shorter each year. He could not compete with the large toy stores and children asked for more expensive items each year. His main business was candy. Elves prepared candy and fruitcakes for delivery and many of the handmade toys were not requested. Elves still made toys. His main delivery was in Asia, Africa, Australia, and India. The industrialized countries turned Christmas into retail frenzy; with stores opening the day after Thanksgiving. Many times he wanted to stop, take five or ten years rest, but many children still believed in him and he could not let them down.

Sighing heavily, he motioned for Creasy to hand him the metallic box. Taking the box, Santa nodded his head and it opened. "Robbie Johnson, Boulder, Colorado, 1912 East Craig Street, USA," Santa said as he reached inward to remove an envelope that contained a letter written to him many years ago. The letter was written on wide-lined paper, yellowed with age, stained with tears, and creased where it had been lovingly and on many occasions sadly unfolded, folded, unfolded, and folded.

Waving his hand over the envelope, it unsealed itself. Removing the letter, Santa laughed. He stood from his chair and laughed loudly. “Thriddle,” he said softly.

Poof!

“Here Santa,” Thriddle answered. He suddenly appeared beside Santa. Thriddle looked at the letter in Santa’s hand and he began to laugh. Mrs. Claus laughed.

Creasy laughed. All the elves in the workshop stopped working and began to laugh.

"Ho! Ho! Ho!" Santa laughed as he held Robbie's letter upward. "Now here is a child with imagination and honest intentions," he laughed.

"Can we fill Robbie's request?"

"No," Thriddle answered. He pointed toward the letter. "That letter was written December 12, 1960 at 3:22:19 P.M. Mountain Time. We have not made those items in fifty-seven years. One item on his list does not even exist. We cannot fill Robbie's request." He shrugged his shoulders. "Robbie is no longer nine years-old. He is sixty-six years, six months, four days, thirty-four minutes, fifty-two seconds old. Robbie is no longer a little boy."

"Ho! Ho! Ho!" Santa laughed. "There is always a little boy or a little girl in each of us. We will fill it! If we do not have it, we will make it!"

Creasy stepped forward. "Santa we have the hat, guns, paper caps and one pair of boots in warehouse number fourteen. The boots are a size seven and Robbie wore a size six when he wrote the letter. We can adjust the boots so they would fit him at the time he wrote the letter."

"Santa, Elves," Mrs. Claus said laughing. She shrugged her shoulders and pointed toward the letter. "Robbie has an adopted eight year-old son who wears a size six and one-half shoe. The boots do not have to be altered. If Nicholas wears two pair of socks, the cowboy boots will fit!"

"Mrs. Claus, you are the sly one," Santa said. "We will fill Robbie's requests. He is too large to enjoy the items, but his adopted son is just the correct age and size. Ho! Ho! Ho!"

"Not everything," Thriddle said. He pointed toward the letter. "It is a complete package. We cannot fill every item. There are two things we do not have."

Santa stopped laughing, "Problem!"

"I can make one of the items," Creasy suggested. "We have many pair of cowboy boots we never delivered. Boys and girls asked for them, but changed their minds at the last minute. I can take the leather from those boots and make a saddle and bridle. The problem is the pony. Where do we get a pony that looks like Roy Rogers' horse, Trigger?"

"That is a problem," Santa said, "Where do we get a one in seven hundred million six hundred forty-two thousand one hundred eight possible combinations?" He paused, thinking. "It has to be exact."

Poof!

Another elf suddenly appeared beside Santa. "Sorry for the intrusion Santa," Wheeler said. "I checked our information. The original Trigger was named Golden Cloud. There is a mare located in Kingsport, Tennessee USA that is a distant relative of Trigger's sire. The gestation period is an estimated eleven months. She will deliver eight days, fourteen hours and six minutes before Midnight December 24. The only problem is the foal will age and mature rapidly. Robbie will only have fourteen days, eight hours, twenty-two minutes and nine seconds to enjoy him before he outgrows the saddle." He paused. "The mare is for sale and the owner does not know she is expecting. If we hurry, we can purchase her. The sale price is low, only six hundred dollars. She comes with a certificate."

Poof! Poof! Poof! Poof! Poof! Poof! Poof! Poof! Poof!

Nine additional elves appeared. "Santa, your sleigh is ready," one of the elves said. "It will take you less than five seconds to arrive at the Carson Ranch in Kingsport, Tennessee USA. We have attached a horse trailer to the rear of your sleigh. If the reindeer behave themselves, the return ride should be smooth."

"You are not going dressed like that!" Mrs. Claus said irritated. She walked to a closet and returned with a pair of blue denim pants, hiking boots, a brown shirt and a blue windbreaker.

Poof!

"OK boys," Santa said. "We have a quick run to the United States." He was sitting on the front seat of his sleigh and casually released the hand brake. "We are bringing back a horse and I want each one of you to behave yourselves. She has never flown and I do not want any fancy flying, circles, roller coaster turns or otherwise unsafe maneuvers."

The white covering moved from the large snow drift as the four reindeer began to prance to the outside. Running slowly at first, they picked up speed. Suddenly, they were airborne.

Golden Cloud

Santa walked into the horse barn following Mr. Carson. Mr. Carson narrowed his eyes and stared at the white bearded man. What was unusual is his two dogs and four cats followed them and every horse in the barn looked upward when they entered. The mare in the left stall made a whinny noise when the bearded man entered the barn. He walked to her and gently patted her.

"I have never seen that before," Mr. Carson said. "Nellie has never reacted like that. I had hoped to sell her but no one wanted her."

"Why not?" Santa asked, "Hello Nellie." He gently rubbed her neck and she moved closer to him and lowered her head.

"Not sure," Mr. Carson answered. "She just does not seem friendly. Why do you want her?"

"It is a partial Christmas gift," Santa answered. "Perhaps she is not friendly because of her name. Can I change her name?"

"Sure," Mr. Carson answered. "She has never been fully titled and the name Nellie was something I thought up. If you purchase her, you can name her anything you want."

Santa thought carefully. "Let me try some names and see what she likes." He leaned closer. "Snow Flake," he whispered into her ear. There was no reaction.

"Bright Eyes," he whispered into her ear. There was no reaction.

"Princess," he whispered into her ear. There was no reaction.

Santa smiled slyly, "Golden Cloud!" The horse made a whinny noise. The two dogs barked excited and the four cats rubbed against Santa's leg and purred. The other horses in the stable made a whinny noise.

"Golden Cloud it is," Santa laughed. "Ho! Ho! Ho!"

Mr. Carson looked puzzled. "The sale price is six hundred dollars cash. If you purchase her, that price does not include delivery. It will cost an additional one hundred dollars to deliver. It will take me two to three days to arrange delivery and there is an additional charge for boarding those days. The daily charge for boarding is twenty-five dollars a day. That is only for hay and water. If you want oats fed to her that is an additional charge of ten dollars a day?"

Santa turned slowly and frowned. "And you wonder why you never received that G.I. Joe action figure with the jeep and backpack for Christmas?"

Mr. Carson had a puzzled look on his face. He held his hand outward and accepted six one hundred dollar bills. He wrote on a sheet of paper, bill of sale and certificate of ownership, and handed the paper to the white bearded man. "Where and when do you want her delivered?"

Santa smiled slightly. "Delivery has been taken care of. Are we done?"

Mr. Carson paused. The man who purchased Nellie had a familiar sound to his voice. He also looked familiar. Mr. Carson remembered he never received the G.I. Joe toy soldier he wanted for Christmas when he was eight years-old. Santa only brought him clothes and a few toys. He always wanted G.I. Joe and he wrote many letters to Santa Claus asking for it but he never received it. There was something in the tone of the man's voice about delivery being taken care of and his question, 'Are we done?'

Mr. Carson nodded his head.

Poof!

The two dogs barked excited and ran toward the entrance to the barn. They barked loudly and jumped upward in excitement. The four cats also rushed to the entrance to the barn. They too, purred and pawed upward. The horses began to whinny.

The white bearded man was gone!

Mr. Carson ran toward the entrance of the barn. In the distance, he saw something amazing. It was Santa Claus! He could see a sleigh going upward into the sky pulled by four reindeer. Attached to the rear of the sleigh was a horse trailer.

He looked at his hand and the money was still there. Rushing to Nellie's stall, she was gone! In the empty stall was a present. The present was wrapped in blue paper, tied with a red ribbon and there was a large red bow at the top. It was February and there was a Christmas present in her stall with a tag attached with his name... Bruce.

He unwrapped the present to discover a G.I. Joe action figure complete with jeep and backpack. Inside the sealed box was a letter. Tearing open the box, he opened the letter.

Telling those false stories about your best friend Jeff was naughty. I hope you have learned your lesson - Santa Claus.

The return trip was smooth and very, very slow; seven seconds. As Santa approached the large snow drift, the secret covering was open and the reindeer, sleigh and horse trailer glided gently into the entrance. As quickly as the covering was uncovered, it was covered. A stall had been prepared for Golden Cloud and Mrs. Claus and the elves were waiting.

"Naughty! Naughty! Naughty!" Mrs. Claus laughed. "You startled Bruce! He is telephoning all of his friends and telling them Santa Claus visited him in February and brought him a present."

"I did," Santa said laughing as he placed the hand brake and dismounted from his seat on the sleigh. "Come see her. She is beautiful!"

The elves lowered the gate to the horse trailer and Golden Cloud emerged proudly. Mrs. Claus approached her and petted her on the neck and nuzzled her. "Welcome to our home!"

Golden Cloud began to prance around the loading and unloading dock. She walked to the deer and gently nuzzled them. Raising her head, she made a whinny sound.

Mrs. Claus had a serious look on her face. "Is she house broken?"

Little Trigger

"Santa, Elves!" Mrs. Claus said. "How can he enjoy the snow dressed like that?"

The young horse looked downward with sad brown eyes. He was dressed in a red snow suit custom made for him. The snow suit covered his back, chest and neck. Zippered leggings covered his four legs. On each hoof, he wore a snow boot. The snow boots covered his hoofs and zipped upward longer than eight inches. Socks covered both ears and he attempted to walk in the snow but he was dressed too tightly.

"Here," Mrs. Claus said. "I am going to remove everything so you can have fun." She removed the snow suit and Little Trigger began to prance in the snow. He galloped a short distance and stopped. Observing the reindeer, he began to chase them. The reindeer were swift and easily avoided him.

Tiring of the game, the reindeer were airborne. Little Trigger looked puzzled as he watched the deer fly. He attempted to leap into the air, to follow them, but he fell downward into the snow. Unable to follow them, he entered the loading dock area and began to prance.

"Beautiful and very spirited," Santa said.

One of the elves approached Little Trigger and placed a bucket of oats in front of him. He began to eat the oats as Mrs. Claus approached him with a carrot. He made a whinny noise as he accepted the carrot and he remained still as she brushed his mane. Little Trigger was very beautiful; a distant relative and an exact duplicate of Roy Rogers' horse Trigger.

"I am going to miss him," Mrs. Claus said as she leaned downward to brush his mane and then his back. "He makes everything exciting and he is unpredictable at times." She looked upward smiling. "I do not think those three fruitcakes he ate agreed with him."

Santa laughed. "Ho! Ho! Ho! That was funny."

Mrs. Claus rubbed his neck gently and tenderly. "I saw you the moment you were born. You stood right up, took your first step, and fell!"

Santa laughed. "Ho! Ho! Ho!"

Mrs. Claus looked sad. "You only have two more days before Santa delivers you. I know Robbie will love you as much as we do." She hugged his neck as a tear rolled down her left cheek.

"Mrs. Claus," Santa said. "We cannot get attached to the toys."

"He is not a toy!" Mrs. Claus said angered. "He is a member of our family and I do not want him to go!"

Santa shrugged his shoulders. "He will only be gone two weeks."

Mrs. Claus looked puzzled, and then she laughed. "Some Christmas presents are not practical and they are returned or exchanged."

"Exactly," Santa said. "Robbie's request when he was nine years-old made perfect sense to a nine-year old boy. Robbie is no longer nine years-old. What he asked for was impractical then and it is impractical now. There will always be the wonderment of a little boy or a little girl inside each of us. I will give Robbie time to enjoy his belated Christmas presents and then I will exchange one of the gifts or give him a refund."

Mrs. Claus smiled as she wiped tears of joy from her cheeks and then she crinkled her nose. "There is one thing I will not miss for two weeks." She pointed downward.

"Oh that," Santa said. "Hopefully he will be house broken before delivery. I will clean it up. Ho! Ho! Ho!"

"It's finished," Creasy said proudly as Santa approached the saddle. It was beautiful! Creasy used leather from many cowboy boots never delivered. He held upward a black and white photograph. "This photograph was taken of Roy Rogers and Trigger from the movie *My Pal Trigger*. The photograph was taken July 1, 1946 at 1:23:19 P.M. Pacific Time and autographed by Roy Rogers July 10, 1946 at 9:16:22 A.M. Pacific Time. I located the autographed photograph from warehouse number sixteen. It is the last one we have and I matched the design of the saddle and bridle exactly! The actual color was an off brown, trimmed in black and silver, exact color match!"

"Ho! Ho! Ho!" Santa laughed. "You have done an excellent job Creasy. I want you with me when I deliver it."

"That is not possible Santa," Creasy said. "There is not enough room on the sleigh."

"We will make room," Santa said. "I need someone to ride with Golden Cloud's foal. Little Trigger will need someone to talk to him and saddle him. There will be plenty of room."

"Thank you Santa!" Creasy said proudly.

Special Night, Special Time, Special Delivery

The sleigh was packed with gifts, the reindeer prepared and Little Trigger was led into the horse trailer attached to the rear of the sleigh.

Everyone stood silent as they watched a large clock placed in the loading dock. Santa and Mrs. Claus lowered their heads as all of the elves followed. Golden Cloud lowered her head and all the reindeer lowered theirs. Little Trigger was standing inside the horse trailer and he lowered his head. The clock hands moved slowly to the time of 9:43 P.M. Greenwich Mean Time. At exactly 9:43 P.M. the clock stopped. At exactly 9:43 P.M. all time in the world stopped. 9:43 P.M. was the exact time Jesus was born.

Their heads remained lowered. Time started again and the clock hands began to move to 9:43:01 P.M. Greenwich Mean Time. When the clock hands moved to 9:43:10 P.M. all time in the world stopped again.

"Ho! Ho! Ho!" Santa laughed, "Time to go!"

The elves cheered, "Merry Christmas!"

Golden Cloud raised her head and pranced proudly to say goodbye to Little Trigger. Creasy laughed as he petted Golden Cloud and entered the horse trailer. The elves laughed as they closed the door.

"Don't be late!" Mrs. Claus laughed as she hugged Santa. She watched him mount his sleigh and release the hand brake. "You know how congested that air traffic across the Pacific Ocean can be. And do not make any unnecessary stops in Hong Kong. Don't forget that little girl in India! She apologized to her friend and she deserves that doll! I removed her name from your naughty list and added it to your nice list."

She smiled slyly as one of the elves handed her a large package. Carefully, she placed it in the sleigh.

Santa narrowed his eyes. "Who is that for?"

"You know very well who it is for," Mrs. Claus laughed, "Mr. Bruce Carson, Kingsport, Tennessee USA."

"I do not know," Santa said. "Bruce was a very naughty boy growing up."

"He has changed!" Mrs. Claus said sternly. "You cannot be everywhere at once. He is pretending he is you for those little kids at the hospital. Bruce will really be surprised when he reaches into his bag and removes that present with his name on it."

Santa frowned. "What is it?"

Mrs. Claus frowned. "You know very well what it is. He wanted it when he was ten years- old; a James Bond 007 Road Race Set; completely wired, landscaped, all ready to go with six scenic panels. It includes an Aston Martin DB5, tunnel, ejecting car seat and simulated plastic oil slicks." She smiled proudly. "I found it myself in warehouse number forty-seven. In case you were wondering, it is his! He was naughty and you marked him from your nice list fifty-two years ago." She pointed to the present and laughed. "His name tag is still on it."

Santa laughed. "Ho! Ho! Ho! Fasten your seat belt Creasy!"

The eight reindeer began to pull the sleigh and horse trailer slowly and gently to the outside. Suddenly, they were airborne.

Belated Christmas Presents

"Daddy! Daddy! Daddy!" Robert's three adopted children yelled as they jumped onto the bed. "Santa came and he brought you your pony! It's outside and very beautiful!"

Robert rose slowly. "What pony?"

"He is outside on the patio!" Nicholas answered excited. "It is golden and has a saddle!"

Kara frowned, holding her nose. "I do not think he is house broken and I am not cleaning it up!"

"There are presents under the tree addressed to Robbie!" Barry said excited. "Open them!"

Robert and his wife Marsha rose quickly and ran to the patio. Their eyes were widely opened. Standing on the patio was a miniature Trigger. He had a saddle, a bridle, and there were hay bales neatly stacked. Robert unwrapped the presents under the tree addressed to Robbie to discover a Roy Rogers' cowboy hat, Roy Rogers' toy guns, with matching twin holsters, and a pair of Roy Rogers' cowboy boots. Opening a larger package, it was filled with boxes of paper caps; more than enough to chase the bad guys away.

Bam! Bam! Bam!

Someone banged on the front door. Robert walked to the door and opened it to find his neighbor Sam angered. "You can't keep a horse in this neighborhood!" Sam yelled.

"I don't know where it came from," Robert said. "I received the horse and Roy Rogers stuff."

"What Roy Rogers stuff?" Sam asked. "They have not made anything with Roy Rogers' name on it in fifty years! Is it real?"

"I guess so," Robert answered. "Come look at it."

Sam looked at the unopened boxes. "Oh my goodness, those things are worth a fortune. If they are real, they are worth about twenty thousand dollars at auction. Where did they come from?"

"I do not know," Robert answered. "I always wanted them but never got them."

"Daddy," Nicholas said. "Can I ride the horse?"

"Me too?" Barry asked. "Can I put on the hat, boots, guns and ride the horse?"

"Don't forget me!" Kara said excited. "I want to ride the horse!"

"That's Trigger, the smartest horse in the movies," Robert said. "Sure, you can open the packages and ride Little Trigger."

"No! No!" Sam yelled. "You cannot open those Roy Rogers items. They are memorabilia and worth nothing if opened! If you open them you will lose fifteen to twenty thousand dollars!"

Robert was completely puzzled. He looked at the items, he always wanted them. Money, he needed money. Walking to the patio doors, he saw the golden palomino. Looking at the sad faces of his three adopted children, he smiled. "Open them and ride him cowboy!"

"No! No!" Sam yelled. "You just lost twenty thousand dollars! I am calling the police on that horse." He was very upset as he stormed out the front door.

Barry, Kara, and Nicholas laughed as they opened the packages. Nicholas pulled the cowboy boots on but they were slightly too large. "Use two pair of socks," Barry suggested.

Nicholas placed two pair of socks on and pulled on the boots, they fit! Loading the twin guns with paper caps, Robert adjusted the waist belt and placed them in their holsters. Marsha laughed as she handed Nicholas the hat and took his photograph. Nicholas was smiling proudly wearing Walt Disney Cars pajamas and Roy Rogers' pistols, boots and hat. Smiling he walked outside and Robert helped him to mount Little Trigger. The pony began to prance proudly around the backyard as Nicholas held the reins with one hand and fired the paper caps from one gun. "Get out of town bad guys!" he yelled. "Roy Rogers and Little Trigger are here!" Quickly running out of ammunition, he exchanged guns.

Taking turns, and wearing multiple pairs of socks, Barry and Kara placed the Roy Rogers' pistols, boots and hat and rode Little Trigger. They laughed as they rode the pony in their backyard and fired the cap guns; chasing the bad guys out of town.

"Thank you, Santa!" Robert laughed as he watched the excitement of his children.

Unexpected Gifts

Ring! Ring! Ring!

Sandra: "Hello."

Eric: "Sandra, it is Eric. I wanted to telephone you and thank you for the Christmas present but it is very expensive and you should return it."

Sandra: "What present? I have a gift for you but I have not given it yet. I was waiting for dinner."

Eric: "The Hopalong Cassidy wristwatch I always wanted. You gave me a Hopalong Cassidy wristwatch. It is very valuable and I did not open it. You need to return it and get your money back. Where did you get it?"

Sandra: "Not me. I do not even know who this Cassidy person is. I did not give it to you."

Eric: "You do not know who Hopalong Cassidy is? When I was a young boy there were cowboys: Roy Rogers, Gene Autry, The Cisco Kid, The Lone Ranger and my favorite Hopalong Cassidy. He was my favorite and I pretended I was him riding a stick horse. I always wanted a Hopalong Cassidy wristwatch. I wrote Santa letters but I never received it."

Sandra: "Ha, ha, ha. You sound like Robert and his pony. I did not give it to you. It is a reproduction."

Eric: "No it is real! It has his picture on the face, a real leather band, it winds and it was made in America. It looks like it is brand new. I did not open the package."

Sandra: Silence.

Eric: "Sandra, are you there?"

Sandra: "This is strange. I have just been on the internet and I was going to telephone you and thank you for the Christmas present. Thank you. What you gave me is also very valuable."

Eric: "I did not give you a present. I have something for you but it is not expensive, low on cash."

Sandra: "You did not leave that doll under my Christmas tree?"

Eric: "No. What kind of doll. I know you like dolls."

Sandra: "Chatty Cathy."

Eric: "I remember that. It was a doll that walked and talked."

Sandra: "Eric, I always wanted a Chatty Cathy. I also wrote letters to Santa and never received it. It is brand new, never opened. There was another package with batteries. You know, those old batteries they do not make anymore, D+ size. I did a search on the internet. The going price for a used, non-working, Chatty Cathy is over nine hundred dollars. With the original box it came in, the price is one hundred dollars higher." Pause. "I have a brand new one that has never been opened... with batteries."

Eric: "Check the watch! Check the watch! Hopalong Cassidy!"

Sandra: Pause. Pause. "Oh, my goodness! Did you know the Hopalong Cassidy wristwatch is more valuable than The Lone Ranger? It is based on quantity made and a non-working, cracked crystal, worn leather band, Hopalong Cassidy wristwatch is being bid on now. The highest bid posted is twelve hundred dollars."

Eric: Pause. "Sandra, we have items we could sell for over two thousand dollars."

Sandra: Pause. Pause. "I always wanted Chatty Kathy. She looks so beautiful."

Eric: Pause. Pause. "I always wanted a Hopalong Cassidy wristwatch."

Sandra: "Dinner tonight? Pick me up at 6:00 P.M.?"

Eric: "Sure. I had some news to tell you but I can tell you now."

Sandra: "Good news or bad news?"

Eric: "Good. I have been offered a job with the United States Postal Service as an attorney."

Sandra: "I thought they hated you because of your frivolous legal suit for a pony for little Robbie. Ha. Ha. Ha."

Eric: "I thought so to but they love me. My brief was very concise, legally accurate, and the person I spoke to admitted I was correct; I should have won. They loved Robbie's Dillydally, Willy-Nilly, Shilly-Shally Letter to Santa Claus brief. It appears I am some type of legend. They want me."

Sandra: Pause. Pause. "I thought they were angered because they have to deliver those letters to the North Pole."

Eric: "I thought so to but it has excited the Air Force. The plane makes a regular scheduled run to the North Pole for weather. They call it the Santa Claus Mail Run. The weather plane will fly to the North Pole and air drop children's letters to Santa Claus on December 20 and pilots are lining up to volunteer. One of the generals has arranged for children to ride on the plane next year. The kids are from impoverished families and you know someone will read their letters and when the kids return, Santa will have delivered. This is wonderful! I never thought Robbie's dillydally, willy-nilly, shilly-shally letter to Santa Claus would be so positive." Pause. Pause. "I am not charging Robert any additional legal fees and I am returning his original five hundred dollars."

Sandra: Pause. Pause. "Are you going to sell your Hopalong Cassidy wristwatch?"

Eric: Pause. Pause. "Are you going to sell your Chatty Cathy?"

Sandra: "I will see you at 6:00 P.M. Bye!"

Eric: "Bye."

Knock. Knock.

The door opened slightly as Eric was greeted by a unique sound, "Can we go for a walk?" A tall doll walked toward him. Sandra laughed as she picked the doll upward and turned it off. "I want to see that watch!"

Eric held his left wrist outward and looked at the watch. "The exact time, according to my Hopalong Cassidy wristwatch, is 6:02 P.M.," he said proudly.

They both laughed. "I have a suggestion," Sandra said. "Instead of going out to eat, let's stay inside and try to figure out who gave us those presents and why?"

"I am for that," Eric said. He stepped inside and closed the door. "My name is Eric. Nice to meet you Chatty Cathy and yes, we can go for a walk."

Returned Present

Robert and his family had just finished eating dinner when Little Trigger began to make a whinny noise. He pranced proudly around the backyard, looked upward, and made a whinny noise. Robert walked to the patio glass doors as someone knocked on the front door.

Knock. Knock.

The knock was not loud, almost discernible. Nicholas was first to the door and he opened it to see a white bearded man wearing blue denim pants, a brown shirt and a blue windbreaker.

"Good evening, Nicholas," the man said. "Is Robbie, I mean Robert at home?"

Barry and Kara came to the door. "Hello Barry and Kara, is Robert at home?"

Marsha walked to the door. "Hello Marsha, is Robert at home?"

"Yes," Marsha answered. "We just completed dinner and we were preparing to eat desert. We are having apple pie. Would you care to join us?"

"Apple pie does not agree with me," the bearded man answered. "However, if you have any more of those excellent oatmeal cookies, I will join you. I need to speak to Robert." He leaned forward and whispered, "It is about Little Trigger."

Marsha shrugged her shoulders. "We have been expecting you. Please come in. I have a few cookies left. Is milk OK?"

"I have never refused milk and cookies," the bearded man answered. "That sounds wonderful!"

Santa walked into the living room area of the house. It was furnished simply and exactly as he remembered it; clean and comfortable. He followed Marsha into the dining area where Robert was standing. "Sam complained to the police about the horse in our backyard and he told me someone from animal control was to come and take him," Robert said sadly. He motioned for the bearded man to sit down. "We have been expecting you. When will you take him?"

Santa laughed. “Ho! Ho! Ho! There is no need to rush.” He looked toward the patio. Little Trigger was standing near the glass doors looking in. He made a whinny noise when he saw Santa. Santa frowned slightly toward him and made a hush noise with his finger over his lips. Little Trigger nodded his head as Santa sat in an empty chair opposite Robert.

“I do not know where he came from,” Robert explained. “He was here Christmas morning and no one has admitted to bringing him here.”

“Thank you,” Santa said as Marsha placed a plate of oatmeal cookies and a glass of milk in front of him. He took a bite. “Delicious. These are fresh. Marsha you are an excellent cook. They taste exactly like the ones you left for Santa on December 24.” He took a sip of milk. “Have you enjoyed him?”

“Oh yes,” Robert answered. “The kids and I love him very much. I understand the city regulations about large animals.” He looked toward the patio doors. “He is getting larger and will soon outgrow his saddle. Also, he eats like a horse.”

"Ho! Ho! Ho!" Santa laughed. "He will outgrow his saddle in two days, eight hours, twenty-two minutes and nine seconds." He paused. "You know you cannot keep him, it is not practical," he said seriously.

Robert smiled. "I know. I am just concerned about him and I think I will worry about him. Where will he live?"

Santa ate another cookie and drank milk. "It is very nice," he answered. "Lots of room, plenty of food and he will have the best of care. There are many people who will enjoy him." He ate another cookie. "Little Trigger will be very happy and so will you. You received the Christmas presents you always wanted. However, some presents are not always practical and on occasion, must be returned or exchanged."

"How do you know his name?" Kara asked.

"Lucky guess?" Santa asked. He leaned forward, with a serious look on his face. "This is the deal. You keep the saddle and bridle. I pay you for Little Trigger. Name your price, any price!"

"He is not for sale," Robert said. "I did not pay anything for him and it does not seem right to sell him.

If you take care of him, he is yours. I would like to keep the saddle and bridle as a memory."

Santa frowned. "Good counter offer but I am prepared to pay you for him. Name your price, any price!" He paused and leaned forward. "He is a very valuable horse."

Robert stood abruptly. "I don't want money! All I want is to know is if he will be happy. I want your guarantee that he will be happy and live a long life! Are there any other horses where he is going?"

Santa smiled brightly, well-pleased with Robbie's unselfish counter offer. "Just one," he answered as he ate another cookie and drank milk. "Where he will be going there are many people who love him; one person in particular. They will care for him and treat him very well. I accept your price of happiness and a long life. I guarantee Little Trigger will live a very long, long, long happy life. Is it a deal?"

"Accept it," Marsha advised. She looked at the white bearded man. There was something about him. His voice sounded familiar and he looked familiar. She had seen him before but she did not know where. "You know you cannot keep him."

"OK," Robert said. "He is yours at no charge. I get to keep the saddle and bridle and you guarantee that he will be happy and live a long time. When will you take him?"

"Transportation will be arranged to pick him up in two days, eight hours, nineteen minutes and twenty-eight seconds," Santa answered. He smiled slightly. "Are we done?"

Robert nodded his head.

Santa stood. "Wonderful cookies and refreshing ice cold milk, I can never get enough. Thank you for a wonderful visit and you are a shrewd negotiator." He shook his finger toward Robert and laughed, "I give you my personal guarantee Little Trigger will live a long time and always be happy." Turning, he walked to the door.

Robert smiled as he followed Santa. "Thank you," he said slowly as he opened the door. He leaned forward and whispered, "Take him at night so the kids do not see you load him into a horse trailer or a pickup truck. Can you take him sooner? The kids will be real upset and so will I if we wait a few days."

"Good suggestion," Santa whispered. "I can take him tonight when everyone is asleep. I promise there will be no noise."

"Thank you again," Robert said as Santa walked out the opened door and slowly, silently, closed it behind him.

"Daddy! Daddy! Daddy!" Robert's kids yelled, as they jumped on the bed. "Come look what is in the living room!"

Robert and Marsha rose slowly to walk into the living room. Their eyes widened. Placed near the wall was a very ornate saddle stand and placed on the stand was the Little Trigger saddle and bridle. Above the stand on the wall were mounted two framed photographs. One photograph was Roy Rogers riding Trigger from the movie *My Pal Trigger*.

Trigger was rearing into the air. The second photograph was Little Trigger; Nicholas was riding him, wearing the hat, toy guns and boots. Standing beside them was Robert, Marsha, Kara, and Barry. The photograph was framed in such a manner, the saddle was easily seen.

"When was that photograph taken?" Marsha asked. "I do not recall us posing."

"Christmas morning," Barry answered. "I do not recall who took the picture but we were standing around the pony."

"Look at this picture!" Nicholas said excited. "Roy Rogers signed it!"

Robert looked at the photograph. On the bottom right corner it was autographed - *Roy Rogers and Trigger July 10, 1946*. The photograph looked new and the signature looked authentic.

"They are exact duplicates," Marsha said. She pointed to the saddles. "They are exact duplicates."

"So are the horses," Kara added, "Except ours is smaller."

Looking outward to the empty backyard, everyone was sad. "He's gone," Robert said sadly. "I wonder what he is doing."

"Screwdriver, please," Wheeler said as he adjusted a wheel on a wagon.

Little Trigger pranced toward Wheeler. On his back, in addition to a saddle, was a tool pouch. He approached Wheeler and turned left allowing Wheeler to remove the screwdriver. Making adjustments to the wheel, Wheeler returned the screwdriver to its pouch. "Thank you!"

Little Trigger made a whinny noise.

"When will he outgrow the saddle tool pouch?" Mrs. Claus asked. She and Santa were standing observing the elves make toys, candy and fruitcakes.

"Never," Santa answered. "Little Trigger and Golden Cloud will always remain as they are. They will never age, they will never become ill."

"Bad idea," Mrs. Claus said.

"Why?" Santa asked surprised. "It is a wonderful idea! Little Trigger and Golden Cloud are members of our family. We will always be together."

"Not that," Mrs. Claus said. She held her nose and pointed downward. "You should have waited until he was house broken."

"Oh that," Santa said. "I can't think of everything. Ho! Ho! Ho!"

Mrs. Claus laughed. "I'll take care of it."

Santa Claus Mail Run - December 20, 2018

The twelve children were excited as the C-17 Globemaster III United States Air Force weather plane approached the North Pole. "This is very important," General Tate began. "In order to be accurate, we must air drop the letters addressed to Santa at the exact location, ninety degrees north." He turned to the navigator.

"Approaching air drop coordinates," the navigator said. "Estimated time to drop zone is thirty-two seconds."

The children laughed excited and moved upward in their seats.

"The cargo bay contains a special container designed just for the Santa Claus Mail Run," General Tate laughed. "Did everyone write their letter to Santa Claus?"

"Yes! Yes!" the children answered excited.

"Estimated time to drop zone is fifteen seconds," the navigator said.

The children strained to look out the one window. All they could see was snow and ice. "How will Santa find it?" one of the girls asked. She was nine years-old and crippled; wearing a leg brace and clutched a doll tightly. Every child in the plane had physical problems, they were all crippled.

"We have the parachute dyed in the color of blue and there are three flashing lights," General Tate answered proudly. "One light is red and the other two are blue and green."

"Drop zone reached!" the navigator yelled excited. "We are at the earth's northern axis, ninety degrees north and exact center; Santa Claus' home... the North Pole!" He laughed loudly as he pressed a button and the sound of hydraulics activating could be heard. The lower cargo bay door opened as a large metallic box slid downward. The blue parachute opened and the box drifted slowly, gently to the surface. The box rested on the snow as three lights: red, blue and green, blinked.

The children laughed and clapped.

The plane made a slow left turn and returned to pass over the drop zone. "Where is it?" the pilot asked. "We just dropped it. Where is it?"

The copilot looked out the window. All he could see was snow and ice. "It should be there and easy to see." He turned to the navigator, "Equipment malfunction?"

"No," the navigator answered. "It was released." He looked at a setting. "Correction, equipment malfunction, the lights are not activating."

"What's wrong?" General Tate whispered. He leaned toward the navigator. "Where is it? I don't see it."

"Not sure," the navigator answered. "It released fine, the parachute opened and the lights activated but it's not there. The lights must have malfunctioned because they have stopped working. The only possible explanation is it landed in water and sank."

General Tate sighed. He turned to the children. "It will take us about thirty minutes to return to the base. There is a big party waiting and Santa may have already received your letters and answered them."

"I wrote Santa I want a new leg brace," a girl nine years-old said. "Not for me but for my best friend Angela." She turned to a girl sitting beside her. The girl looked sad. "Mine does not work so well. It is too heavy and it pinches when I walk."

General Tate frowned as he turned to one of the female officers. "Where did that request come from?" he whispered. "All we saw in those letters was toys and clothes."

"No idea," the officer whispered back. "We will have one disappointed child. We can get her friend a new leg brace but it will take time." She shrugged her shoulders.

The children laughed as the plane flew toward the base.

Santa Stops Time!

"Special air mail delivery for Santa!" Creasy yelled. "Special air mail delivery for Santa!"

The elves were excited and cheered as Creasy and many others returned from retrieving the box. Santa laughed as he walked to the large metallic box. He nodded his head and it opened. Many elves climbed inside and began to pass letters. "Boy, girl, girl, boy," one elf said as he removed sealed envelopes addressed to: Santa Claus, North Pole. Each letter had a cancelled stamp.

One elf took letters written from girls and placed them in a special mail pouch attached, like a saddle, to Little Trigger. When the mail pouch was filled, Little Trigger pranced to the main section of the work shop where one elf removed the letters and passed them out. He returned to the loading dock to receive more letters.

Golden Cloud was larger and her mail saddle pouch was also larger. Letters written from boys were packed tightly in the mail pouch and she pranced proudly to the main work shop to deliver them.

The elves were busy receiving and filling orders. Santa and Mrs. Claus laughed as the entire work shop was busy.

"Problem Santa," Wheeler said, as he approached Santa. He handed him a letter.

Santa took the letter and stared at the unsealed envelope. He breathed a heavy sigh and lowered his head. All the elves stopped working and looked toward Santa and they also sighed heavily. Mrs. Claus had a very sad look on her face.

Golden Cloud and Little Trigger also had sad looks on their faces as the reindeer lowered their heads.

"I can fill it," Wheeler said. "The only problem is time. The plane is scheduled to return to the base in six minutes, fourteen seconds."

"How much time do you need?" Santa asked as he raised his head.

"Fourteen hours, eight minutes and eleven seconds," Wheeler answered. "I have a replacement leg brace for Karen's friend Angela but it does not work correctly. I know her measurements but this is very delicate work. I will have to completely dismantle the brace and replace some parts. There are engineering and manufacturing defects that must be corrected." He lowered his head. "I am sorry."

"Time, I need more time," Wheeler added sadly, as a tear rolled slowly down his left cheek.

Santa lowered his head and sighed heavily. Everyone was saddened.

Golden Cloud began to whinny. She reared upward and made a loud whinny sound. Scraping her right hoof against the floor, she reared upward and made a whinny sound. She turned toward the loading dock and ran in a gallop. Stopping at the end of the work shop she reared upward.

Little Trigger, understanding his mother, also made a whinny noise and reared upward. He galloped to stand beside his mother, near the entrance to the loading dock, and made a whinny noise.

"The clock!" Mrs. Claus said excited. "Santa can use the Christmas Clock to stop time!"

Poof! Poof! Poof! Poof! Poof! Poof! Poof! Poof! Poof! Poof! Poof! Poof! Poof! Poof! Poof! - And many, many, many more poofs!

Santa was standing in front of the Christmas Clock. He reached for it and manually adjusted the time. He sped the clock hands forward, one day, two days, three days and four days. Everyone lowered their heads. The clock hands moved slowly to the time of 9:43 P.M. At exactly 9:43 P.M. the clock stopped. At exactly 9:43

P.M. all time in the world stopped. 9:43 P.M. was the exact time Jesus was born.

Their heads remained lowered. Time started again and the clock hands began to move to 9:43:01 P.M. When the clock hands moved to 9:43:10 P.M. all time in the world stopped again.

"Ho! Ho! Ho!" Santa laughed. "Take all the time you need Wheeler." Wheeler was not present; he was busy preparing and repairing the leg brace.

All work in Santa's work shop had stopped. Every elf waited patiently for Wheeler to prepare the gift; the one gift Santa stopped time for; the unselfish gift.

Fourteen hours, eight minutes and eleven seconds later, it was finished. Santa moved the Christmas Clock hands backward to six minutes, fourteen seconds before the plane was scheduled to return to the base. Mrs. Claus breathed a sigh of relief. "That was close," she said. She turned to Santa. "What are you waiting for? You had better hurry."

Santa laughed. "Ho! Ho! Ho! I have already delivered." He offered her a cookie. "They taste real good, oatmeal raisin."

Mrs. Claus and the elves laughed. Little Trigger and Golden Cloud made a whinny sound as the reindeer made noises. The elves continued to laugh as they returned to their work, filling orders.

"Very tasty," Mrs. Claus said as she ate the cookie.

"Group photo!" one of the elves yelled. "Group photo!"

"Everyone smile! Say Candy Cane!"

"Candy Cane!" Santa, Mrs. Claus, and the elves said. Little Trigger waved as the deer made noises.

FLASH!

The Last Present

Colonel Parker entered the United States Air Force dining hall. He was dressed as Santa Claus, complete with false beard. The children cheered and everyone clapped as he carried his bag filled with gifts. One end of the dining hall was decorated with a large Christmas tree and a chair. Beside the chair was a table with an empty plate of cookies and an empty glass of milk placed on top. He waved as he walked to the chair and sat. Many soldiers were dressed as elves and laughed excited.

Colonel Parker had been told of the little girl's letter to Santa Claus. He laughed sadly as he reached into his bag to retrieve a present, called out the name, and one of the elves handed out the present.

The children laughed as they opened their presents to find exactly what they wrote Santa for; toys and clothes. The only child who did not have a present was Karen. Her request was a present, not for herself, but for her best friend Angela.

He reached to the table for the plate of cookies and the cookies were all gone. Puzzled, he reached for the glass of milk to find the glass empty. Angered that someone ate his cookies and drank his milk, he reached to his bag to find it also empty. All the presents had been given out, there was nothing for Karen. Shrugging his shoulders sadly, he stood.

"There is one present left," one of the female officers, dressed as Mrs. Santa Claus, said. She pointed toward the tree. Colonel Parker looked where she pointed. Leaning against the wall behind the decorated Christmas tree was a large box. The box was wrapped in green paper, tied with red ribbon and a very large red bow was placed at the top. The box was not there when he helped to decorate the tree. He never saw it and it was big! Walking to the box, he looked puzzled at the name on the tag... to Angela from your best friend Karen.

Turning slowly, he picked it up. Although the box was large and looked heavy, what was in it was as light as a feather. It felt like the box was empty.

"This present is for Angela from your best friend Karen," he said curiously. He walked to Angela and placed it in front of her. Carefully, she began to unwrap it.

"What is it?" one of the doctors asked. His eyes widened as the item was revealed... a Gemini Mark 16

Aircraft Aluminum-Silicate Structured Prosthetic - Youth Size Six.

Walking to Angela, the doctor carefully removed her old leg brace and replaced it with the new one. Angela laughed as she stood and walked. “It is so light and the sides do not pinch!” She walked to Karen. “Thank you Karen!” Angela said, as she hugged Karen, “Merry Christmas!”

“You are very welcome and Merry Christmas,” Karen said as she returned Angela’s hug.

Everyone in the cafeteria clapped.

“Where did that come from?” General Tate asked the doctor. “Do not worry about the cost; we will take care of the cost. How did you know?”

“That thing doesn’t work,” the doctor whispered. “There are all kinds of engineering and manufacturing problems with it.”

General Tate frowned. “Are you drinking? We all agreed not to drink alcoholic beverages, smoke or use inappropriate language around the children.” He observed Angela walking and laughing. “It works fine.”

"No it doesn't," the doctor whispered. "It locks when a child takes six to seven steps. The aircraft aluminum is a new silicon-based alloy. It is very light in weight but there are problems with the connections. One of the problems is the new alloy resists friction and grabs; causing the connections to lock." He looked to General Tate. "I am not drinking but I need a drink. Somebody fixed it!"

General Tate laughed. "So, there were problems and somebody fixed it. What difference does it make?"

"That device will allow more than ten thousand crippled children to have greater mobility because of its light weight," the doctor whispered. "The Gemini Mark 16 was initiated and funded by the United Nations for impoverished crippled children in Africa, India, and Haiti. It was scheduled to be abandoned because it did not work. Somebody fixed it!" He laughed loudly. "I need a drink to celebrate and I want that child's brace so we can see how it was repaired."

General Tate turned to the doctor. "Soldier, are you telling me you want to take a leg brace from a crippled child at Christmas?" He smiled slightly. "Somebody fixed it and more than ten thousand poor crippled children in

Africa, India, and Haiti will have greater mobility? Hum. I will arrange for another one for her to use to allow you to examine it. However, we will take care of that after Christmas." He frowned and leaned toward the doctor. "It is hers! You are not taking it from her and you are not going to dismantle it. You will not remove one nut, one bolt or one cotter pin, that's a direct order!"

"Yes, Sir!" the doctor said as he stood to attention and saluted. "It does not have cotter pins."

"Good!" General Tate said angered. "I will give you exactly one week, or seven days, or one hundred sixty-eight hours, or ten thousand eighty minutes to examine it after Christmas; not one second more."

General Tate leaned upwards and smiled brightly. "At ease soldier, if you need more time, send me an official request. Considering the unique circumstances and the possible outcome of your examination, I am certain the little girl will co-operate." He made a grunt sound and turned to observe the children; they were playing a game with one of the soldiers dressed as an elf. Angela was laughing as she played a game where a present is passed from child to child; music is played, and then stopped.

The general continued to observe the girl laughing as she and many others played the game. Her motions appeared almost normal. The leg brace she wore worked without flaw as she laughed and walked.

General Tate smiled and laughed. "You are correct, somebody fixed it." He turned to the doctor. "You will not celebrate alone, that is an order," he whispered. "We will all celebrate with you after the children leave. That also is an order. No alcoholic beverages, the milk and the soda drinks are on me."

Colonel Parker walked to the female officer dressed as Mrs. Santa Claus. "Did you eat my cookies and drink my milk?"

Christmas Eve - December 24, 2018

The sleigh was packed with gifts, the reindeer prepared and everyone stood silent as they watched a large clock placed in the loading dock. Santa and Mrs. Claus lowered their heads as all of the elves followed. Golden Cloud and Little Trigger lowered their heads and all the reindeer lowered theirs. The clock hands moved slowly to the time of 9:43 P.M. Greenwich Mean Time. At exactly 9:43 P.M. the clock stopped. At exactly 9:43 P.M. all time in the world stopped. 9:43 P.M. was the exact time Jesus was born.

Their heads remained lowered. Time started again and the clock hands began to move to 9:43:01 P.M. Greenwich Mean Time. When the clock hands moved to 9:43:10 P.M. all time in the world stopped again.

"Ho! Ho! Ho!" Santa laughed, "Time to go!"

The elves cheered, "Merry Christmas!"

Golden Cloud and Little Trigger pranced proudly around the loading dock, making a whinny sound. The reindeer were excited and they made noises.

"I have not seen that sleigh packed with so many gifts in many years," Mrs. Claus said.

"Twenty-three years to be exact," Santa said proudly. "Things are changing for the better. More children than last year believe in me and adults are starting to believe in me also." He turned to Mrs. Claus and hugged her. "Robbie's dillydally, willy-nilly, shilly-shally letter to me has affected many people. My nice list is very long and many of the gifts I will deliver tonight are unselfish."

Mrs. Claus smiled proudly and waved as Santa mounted his sleigh and released the hand brake. "We have a long night ahead of us," Santa said. "I want you boys to have fun! I want to see fancy flying, circles and roller coaster turns." The deer made noises as the heavy sleigh was pulled from the loading dock. Running slowly at first, the reindeer ran faster and they were airborne. They flew straight upward, completed fifteen roller coaster turns, nineteen loops, twelve backward flips, and headed south east, toward India. Santa's sleigh approached from the north east from Canada, returning as quickly as it left. The sleigh was empty. Santa set the hand brake, stepped down from his seat, and stretched his legs and back. "That was a long night!"

Mrs. Claus was waiting impatiently and tapped her foot. "What took you so long?"

Golden Cloud and Little Trigger made a whinny noise. Little Trigger pranced to the rear of the sleigh and made motions with his head. The elves giggled and the reindeer made noises.

Santa smiled slightly. "Tattle tells," he muttered as he reached into the rear compartment of the sleigh and removed a trophy.

Mrs. Claus crossed her arms and frowned. "I know what you did! You started time and then stopped it. Well! Did you get third place again?"

"No," Santa answered proudly. He held upward the trophy:

FIRST PLACE

ANNUAL SANTA CLAUS LOOK-ALIKE CONTEST

SANTA CLAUS, INDIANA USA

DECEMBER 24, 2018

Mrs. Claus laughed. "You have been in that annual contest for ten years and never won."

"Twelve years to be exact," Santa said. "Ho! Ho! Ho! That was much fun."

"What did you do different this year that you did not do before?" Mrs. Claus asked.

"It was my laugh," Santa answered seriously. "This year I am happier than before. The judges liked my laugh. Ho! Ho! Ho!"

The elves laughed and Golden Cloud and Little Trigger made a whinny sound. The reindeer made noises.

Mrs. Claus laughed. "No more February post-Christmas let down?"

"Mrs. Claus, I am going to be too busy preparing my nice list to fool with that," Santa answered. "News about the first United States Air Force Mail Air Drop to me at the North Pole on December 20 is being reported in China and the Soviet Republics." He reached into his coat pocket and removed a thick roll of paper. Holding one end, the rolled paper fell to the floor and began to unroll. It unrolled along the length of the loading dock floor, through the main workshop, turned left toward the dining hall and continued unrolling.

"Do you want to know how many nice children there are in China?"

"Lots of overtime!" one of the elves yelled excited.

Acknowledgements

The importance of a company is judged by its products, its knowledgeable staff and the value and reputation of its marks. The following products, and or, services are registered trademarks, trademarks, or service marks of their respective companies, and or, countries:

Aston Martin DB5

C-17 Globemaster III

Cars

Chatty Cathy

Cracker Barrel

Gene Autry

G.I. Joe

Golden Cloud

Hopalong Cassidy

James Bond 007

Robbie's Letter to Santa Claus

Lionel

Roy Rogers

The Cisco Kid

The Lone Ranger

Trigger - The Smartest Horse in the Movies

United Nations

United States Air Force

United States Postal Service

Walt Disney

References

James, 145 AD, *The Protoevangelium of James. Ante-Nicene Fathers*, Vol. 8. (1886), Buffalo, NY: Christian Literature Publishing Co.

As Mary gave birth, Joseph experienced all activity around him momentarily suspended; birds stiffened while flying in the air and did not fall. One interpretation of the gospel account of James, the half-brother of Jesus, is God stopped time when Jesus was born.

www.ingramcontent.com/pod-product-compliance
Lightning Source LLC
Chambersburg PA
CBHW070620310726
48982CB00001B/133

* 9 7 8 0 9 8 9 9 2 6 5 6 0 *